At the Park

By Jenna Lee Gleisner

SPARKS

Picture Glossary

climb 6

hang 8

slide 14

swing 4

I like the park.

I swing at the park.

swing

I like the park.

I climb at the park.

climb

I like the park.

I hang at the park.

hang

I like the park.

I dig at the park.

dig

I like the park.

I run at the park.

run

I like the park.

I slide at the park.

slide

Do You Know?

What does he do at the park?

swing | climb | hang

dig | run | slide